Based on the original Paddington Bear stories by

Michael Bond

Paddington's Christmas Post

Illustrated by R. W. Alley

HarperCollins *Children's Books*

One crisp morning, Paddington hurried over to the Portobello
Market to see the Christmas decorations. Ever since he'd
heard they were going up, he'd thought of very little else, and he
wasn't disappointed. Brightly coloured shapes and fairy lights hung

in the windows and it all looked most inviting.
But Paddington had another reason for going
shopping and he needed to talk to his friend Mr Gruber . . .

Mr Gruber led the way to the back of his shop
for their elevenses.

"Is everything all right, Mr Brown?" he asked.

"I'm saving to buy Christmas presents,"
explained Paddington sadly, "but I haven't
enough for anything special."

Mr Gruber handed him a steaming mug of cocoa.
"There is a lot of truth in the old sayings," he said,
"and never more so than 'It's the thought that counts'."
"Thank you, Mr Gruber," said Paddington,
sipping his cocoa thoughtfully.
"That gives me an idea."

When Paddington got
back to number thirty-two
Windsor Gardens, Judy
handed him a package
with Peruvian stamps on
it. "It's from Aunt Lucy,"
she said.

Paddington Brown

32 Windsor Gardens

London W2

United Kingdom

the Home for
Retired Bears
LIMA, PERÚ

Each morning Paddington
hurried downstairs to open
a new window on his
calendar, but the more he
opened the further away
Christmas seemed.

However, there was plenty to keep
Paddington busy, for he was making
his own Christmas cards.

   "I don't suppose many people get
cards from a bear," said Mrs Bird,
pretending not to notice the
marmalade stains.

Next Paddington helped
Jonathan and Judy with
some Christmas cookies.
But there was soon
a strong smell
of burning.

"Baking isn't as easy as it looks,"
said Paddington, "especially with paws."
"Never mind," said Judy. "You did your best."

Just then Mr Brown arrived home
with a huge Christmas tree.
  "Perhaps I could help?"
offered Paddington excitedly.
"Bears are good at putting
up decorations."

Apart from the tree, there were fairy lights, tinsel and holly to be put up and large bells made of crinkly paper.

Together they did most of the house, and Paddington found that having thick fur was very useful when it came to hanging up the prickly holly.

By the time they had finished, the house had taken on quite a festive air and everyone gathered to admire Paddington's hard work.

"Well, I must say it's a lovely sight," said Mrs Brown amid general agreement.

"And I found just the place for my cookies," said Paddington.

Shortly afterwards, Paddington had a very
important letter to write to Santa Claus.

Carefully sealing the envelope,
he hid it up the chimney.

BY PAW

Santa Claus

The North Pole

Announcing that he was busy, Paddington disappeared into his room early on Christmas Eve, taking with him an assortment of craft supplies. "Whatever is he doing in there?" wondered Jonathan.

At last it was Christmas morning and Paddington was astonished
to find a pillowcase bulging with parcels at the end of his bed.
His eyes grew larger as he unwrapped them.
It was very strange, but everything
on his list was there!

Aunt Lucy
Home for Retired Bears
Lima
Peru
South America

Being a bear, Paddington has two birthdays, one in the summer
and one on Christmas Day, and Mr Gruber had been invited for
lunch, as Paddington's guest of honour.

After they had eaten, Mr Gruber turned to Paddington.
"I have a small present for you," he said.
A gasp went up as Paddington tore the paper off,
for it was a beautiful scrapbook with his
name on the cover.

"Thank you, I shall only put my best adventures in here," said Paddington. "I have a surprise for each of you too. Follow me . . ."

Under the tree were six gifts.

"I made them all myself," said Paddington, "but I hope you like them."

"We all seem to be very lucky," said Mrs Brown.

"I'm sorry about yours, Mrs Bird," he added. "I had trouble with the paper."

"An ornament!" exclaimed Mrs Bird. "And it's shaped like a bear – how lovely! I can't think of a nicer present."

"So that's what you were doing!" said Jonathan.

"Yes," said Paddington. "It was Mr Gruber who gave me the idea."

That evening Paddington took an extra slice of Christmas pudding upstairs in case he got hungry during the night. But first he wanted to write to his Aunt Lucy.

Aunt Lucy
Home for Retired Bears
Lima
Peru
South America

AIR MAIL

Paddington climbed into bed and opened his new scrapbook.
He wanted to write down everything while it was still fresh
in his mind. "I think," he said to himself, "it has been
such a lovely day – I would like to have
Christmas every year!"

But before he could write a word his eyes closed,
followed by the sound of gentle snoring.

First published in hardback in Great Britain by HarperCollins*Publishers* Ltd in 2022

1 3 5 7 9 10 8 6 4 2

ISBN: 978-0-00-841326-2

HarperCollins *Children's Books* is a division of HarperCollins*Publishers* Ltd
1 London Bridge Street, London SE1 9GF

www.harpercollins.co.uk

HarperCollins*Publishers*, 1st Floor, Watermarque Building, Ringsend Road, Dublin 4, Ireland

Printed in China